P9-CRT-285

USA VALENCIA 3487

San Francisco Public Library
FOR COMMUNITY USE
NOT FOR RESALE
Withdrawn from authorized by SFPL

Henry the Boy

story by Molly Felder
illustrations by Nate Christopherson & Tara Sweeney

penny candy BOOKS

Penny Candy Books
Oklahoma City & Savannah

Text © 2019 Molly Felder
Illustrations © 2019 Nate Christopherson & Tara Sweeney

All rights reserved. Published 2019. Printed in Canada.

 This book is printed on paper certified to the environmental and social standards of the Forest Stewardship Council™ (FSC®).

Photo of Molly Felder: Jim Felder
Photo of Nate Christopherson & Tara Sweeney: Siri Knutson
Design: Shanna Compton

23 22 21 20 19   1 2 3 4 5
ISBN-13: 978-0-9996584-0-6 (hardcover)

Small press. Big conversations.
www.pennycandybooks.com

3 1223 12870 3510

*To my father and friend, Jim Felder, for whom
I have always been Molly the Girl.*

Underneath my shark and dinosaur and bird stickers, my crutches went *click-click-click* down the stairs to breakfast.

With my crutches, I was Henry the heron.

At school, I lined up behind Joel. He said, "Hi!"
My crutches went *click-click-click* on the floor.

Olive shouted, "Henry is a robot!"

I didn't feel like a heron anymore.

I handed Joel my crutches. But I couldn't
move my feet without them.

I put my arms in the cuffs again.

"Do I walk like a robot, Joel?"

"More like a chicken," he said.

"That's a bad friend answer," I said.

I went *click-click-click* away from Joel and into the boys' bathroom.

I looked in the mirror and
tried to stand straighter.

But I stood like me.

One of my crutches
slipped away.

And
Smack!
I fell.

Joel heard me yell "Ow!"

He came to help.

My legs felt weird,
like they belonged
to a robot.

At recess, he showed me
his sponge dinosaur.

"It was supposed to grow
in water, but it didn't. I'm
sorry you fell, Henry."

I named the dinosaur
Audrey. I put her on top of
my crutches while Joel and
I took turns on the slide.

After recess, I went
click-click-click inside,
with Audrey in my pocket.

"Can you come to my house?"
I asked Joel.

And he did.

He rolled around on the grass.
I threw down my crutches and rolled like him.

"Why did you do that?" Joel said.

"I want to play without my crutches."

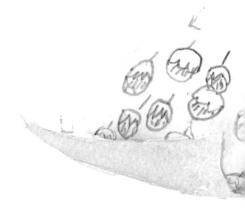

Audrey attacked our cars in the
mud until we were all dirty.

Mom opened the back door.
"Snack time!"

I tucked Audrey back in my
pocket. I pulled my crutches
close.

"You can do it," Joel said.

I put my muddy arm into one cuff
and pressed the crutch down.

Click.

And then I stood up.

After we ate, Joel went home.
I needed a bath.

I went *click-click-click* up each stair

and introduced Audrey to my
octopus and my bathtub shark.

After Audrey and I were clean,
I went *click-click-click* over to
my bookshelf.

I sat down with her and my big book of
animals, but I told her my own story.

Not about a heron or a robot
or a chicken. About me—
Henry the boy.

MOLLY FELDER has a physical disability called cerebral palsy. Her assistance dog, Patterson, was placed with her through Canine Companions for Independence. He helps her by opening doors, turning lights on and off, and much more. In 2016, they attended the Highlights Foundation Kids' Book Revision Retreat together in beautiful Honesdale, Pennsylvania. Molly received her MA from New York University's Gallatin School of Individualized Study, where she focused on creative writing and disability culture. She is committed to representing children of all abilities in her writing, and loves teaching English to Chinese students online. She lives in Alabama.

TARA SWEENEY and **NATE CHRISTOPHERSON** are a mother-and-son team who combine watercolor with ink to create magical illustrations. *A to Zåäö: Exploring the American Swedish Institute* (University of Minnesota Press, 2019) is their debut picture book. *Henry the Boy* is their second collaboration. Nate earned a BA in studio art from Saint Olaf College and an MA in special education from Augsburg University in Minnesota. He teaches special education. Tara earned BS degrees in art and design from the University of Wisconsin and an MFA from the Minneapolis College of Art and Design. She is professor emeritus at Augsburg University. As artists and educators Nate and Tara are committed to cultivating curiosity. They live in Saint Paul, Minnesota.